9-11-09

Yummy in My Tummy

Published in 2009 by Windmill Books, LLC
303 Park Avenue South, Suite # 1280, New York, NY 10010-3657

Series Editor: Nick Turpin
Design: Robert Walster
Production: Jenny Mulvanny
Series Consultant: Gill Matthews

Publisher Cataloging Data

Harrison, Paul, 1969-
       Yummy in my tummy! / Paul Harrison and Belinda Worsley.
              p. cm. – (Get ready)
       Summary: Simple text and colorful illustrations tell about a fly enjoying all of
its favorite foods until it becomes a tasty meal.
       ISBN 978-1-60754-263-6
       1. Flies—Juvenile fiction   2. Food—Juvenile fiction   [1. Flies—Fiction
2. Food—Fiction]   I. Worsley, Belinda   II. Title   III. Series
       [E]—dc22

Manufactured in the United States of America

Yummy in My Tummy

Paul Harrison
and Belinda Worsley

alphabet
soup™

an imprint of

WINDMILL
BOOKS™
New York

"I'm hungry," said Fly.

5

"Mmm, pizza.
Yummy in my tummy."

6

"Mmm, French fries.
Yummy in my tummy."

8

9

"Mmm, dog food.
Yummy in my tummy."

10

"Mmm, chips.
Yummy in my tummy."

13

"Mmm, soda.
Yummy in my tummy."

15

BURP!

17

"Time for dessert!"

18

19

"Mmm, pudding.
Yummy in my tummy."

20

"Mmm, chocolate.
Yummy in my tummy."

"Mmm, doughnuts.
Yummy in my tummy."

24

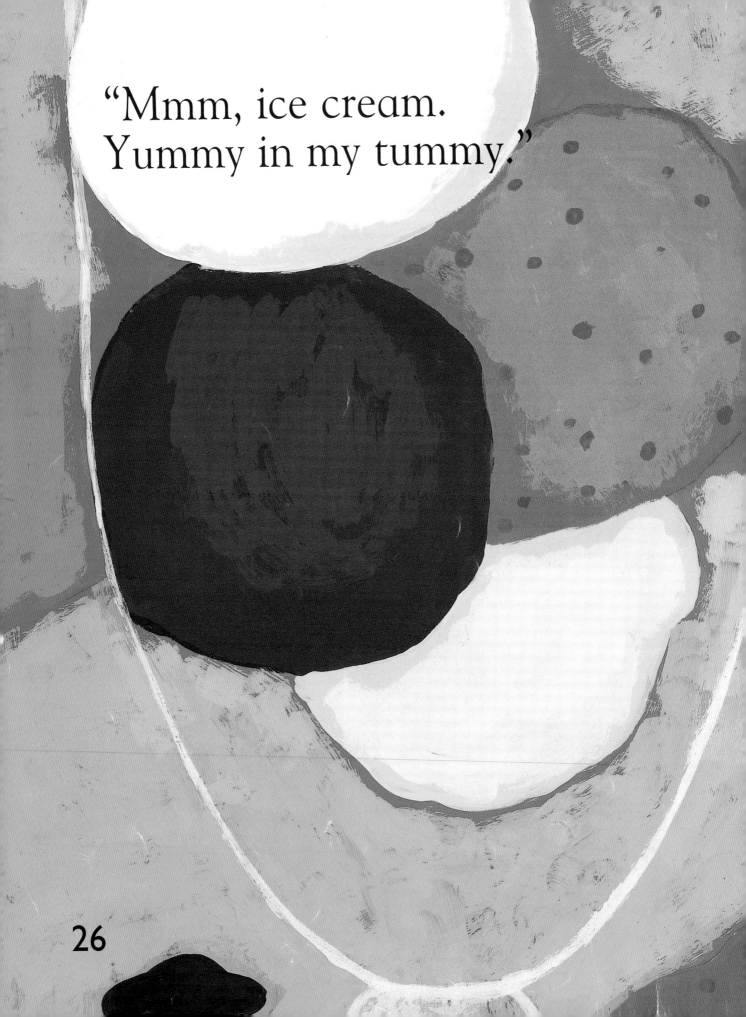

"Mmm, ice cream.
Yummy in my tummy."

26

27

THWAP!

29

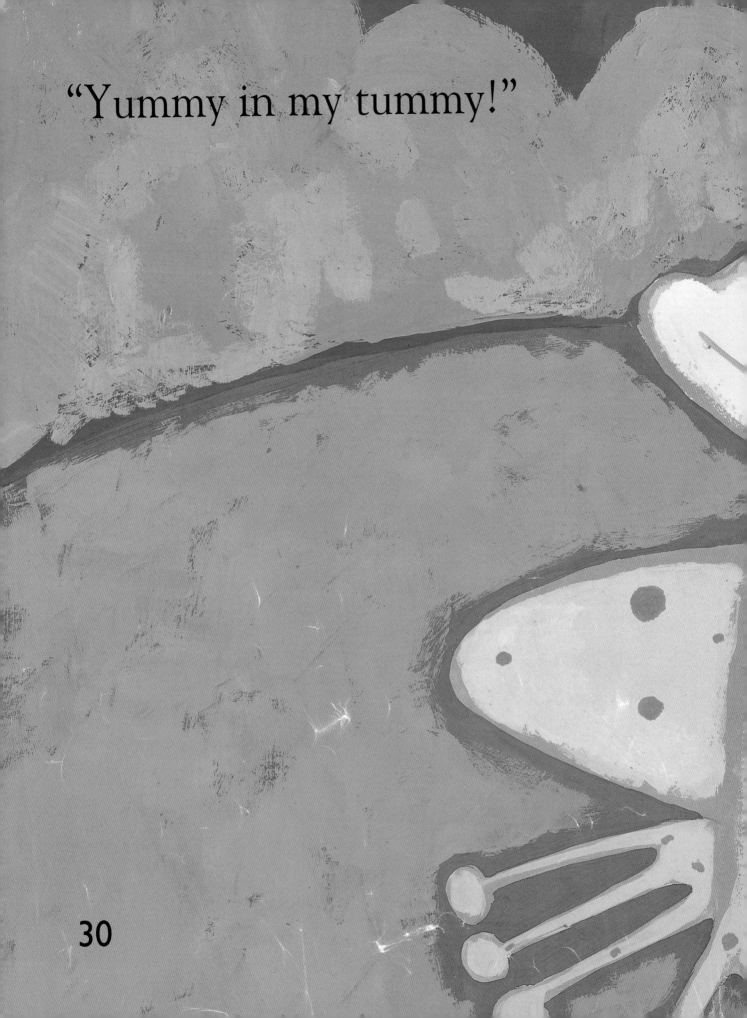

"Yummy in my tummy!"

30

For more great fiction and nonfiction, go to www.windmillbks.com.